W9-BWW-700

BLIND OUTLAW

Holiday House Books
Written and Illustrated by Glen Rounds

OL' PAUL, THE MIGHTY LOGGER

LUMBERCAMP

PAY DIRT

THE BLIND COLT

STOLEN PONY

RODEO

WHITEY AND THE RUSTLERS

HUNTED HORSES

WHITEY AND THE BLIZZARD

BUFFALO HARVEST

LONE MUSKRAT

WHITEY TAKES A TRIP

WHITEY ROPES AND RIDES

WHITEY AND THE WILD HORSE

WHISTLEPUNK OF CAMP 15

WHITEY'S FIRST ROUNDUP

WILD ORPHAN

WHITEY AND THE COLT-KILLER

WHITEY'S NEW SADDLE

THE TREELESS PLAINS

THE PRAIRIE SCHOONERS

WILD HORSES OF THE RED DESERT

ONCE WE HAD A HORSE

THE COWBOY TRADE

THE DAY THE CIRCUS CAME TO LONE TREE

WILDLIFE AT YOUR DOORSTEP

MR. YOWDER AND THE LION ROAR CAPSULES

THE BEAVER: HOW HE WORKS

MR. YOWDER AND THE STEAMBOAT

MR. YOWDER AND THE GIANT BULL SNAKE

MR. YOWDER, THE PERIPATETIC SIGN PAINTER:
   THREE TALL TALES

BLIND OUTLAW

written and illustrated by

Glen Rounds

Holiday House, New York

Library of Congress Cataloging in Publication Data

Rounds, Glen, 1906-
    Blind outlaw.

    SUMMARY: A blind outlaw horse is tamed by a boy who
can not speak.
    1. Horses—Legends and stories. [1. Horses—Fiction.
2. Mutism—Fiction. 3. Physically handicapped—Fiction]
I. Title.
PZ10.3.R76Bm   [Fic]   80-15848
    ISBN 0-8234-0423-4

For Margery, with love

Contents

Oddly enough, during all the long summer the Boy and the Blind Outlaw were around the ranch, neither was ever known by name.

The Boy had some sort of impediment in his speech and could only make wordless sounds. So while he most probably did have a name, there was no way of knowing what it was.

And if in his mind the Boy had a name for the Horse, it stayed as much a mystery as his own.

To this day when their story is told, they are simply called The Boy and the Blind Outlaw.

1
The
Horse

I⊤ ᴡᴀꜱ about the middle of a late spring morning when the Horse came in sight from the far side of the bare ridge and stood for a while on the highest part.

He appeared to be four or five years old, compactly built and with a rough coat somewhere between blue-gray and mouse color. He wore no owner's brand, and the only distinctive mark on him was the strange mask-like patch of darker color covering his forehead and upper muzzle. The untidy tangles and mats of cockleburs and mud in his long tail and mane marked him as a range horse, and not one that had simply strayed off from some ranch or farm.

For a time he stood quietly on the crest with his head held high, his sharply pointed ears flicking forward and back as he snuffed through widened nostrils, testing the tiny air currents that drifted up the sun-warmed slope from the flat below.

The faint sound of magpies quarreling came from somewhere out of sight, and nearby a big fly buzzed loudly as he went about his morning's business. There was a smell of sage and old winter grass as well as the fainter scent of newly turned earth from where a gopher was repairing or enlarging his burrow.

But none of these things appeared to disturb the Horse, and before long he started unhurriedly down the slope.

He moved with a certain caution, his steps almost catlike as he set each hoof carefully down before moving the next. With his head held low,

he seemed to be intent on each small sound or scent coming to him from the grass ahead.

Nonetheless he walked without hesitation, and from a little distance a bystander would not have known that the Horse was blind. Apparently, with long practice, he had learned to "read" the world around him with surprising accuracy by scent and sound instead of by sight.

Coming down onto the little flat where the first green grass was just beginning to appear in small scattered patches, the Blind Horse began to graze. Pushing his muzzle deep among the last year's stems, he sniffed out the hidden tender tufts without trouble, greedily cropping each one, then moving on in search of the next.

But as he fed, his ears and nose continually brought him news from both close by and far off. He took no notice when an early rising grasshopper flew out from under his nose with a sudden raspy whir. Nor was he startled by the occasional quick scurryings of field mice in nearby tussocks.

But when a rattlesnake, sunning himself on a nearby patch of bare ground, wakened and started slowly gathering his coils, the Horse threw up his head at the first dry scaly rustle. With his ears pointing stiffly forward, he quickly located the source of the small sounds, and identified the snake by his rank scent.

Since the snake was out of striking distance, the Horse stood without moving—but listening intently. And for a little while the snake seemed to be waiting also. Then, when the Horse made no threatening move, the snake relaxed his coils and began to crawl slowly away in the direction of a nearby patch of buckbrush. Pointing his ears to follow the tiny rustlings as the snake wound his way through the high grass, the Horse waited until both the scent and the sounds had disappeared. Then he went back to his interrupted feeding.

Later in the morning, as the sun warmed the air and set larger air currents drifting lazily this way and that, he caught a faint whiff of the warm

furry scent of a coyote. Unlike the big gray wolves that were still fairly common in that country, the coyote hunted only small creatures, and the Horse seemed to follow the animal's progress with only neighborly interest.

The coyote trotted up to an old buffalo skull some distance from the Horse. After sniffing carefully, he raised a leg and added his mark to the ones already there, then started searching the high grass for his breakfast.

With his nose busily twitching and his big ears braced forward to catch the slightest scurry or rustle in the grass, the coyote moved stealthily from tussock to tussock. The Horse continued to stand quietly where he was, following the coyote's progress by the strengthening or weakening of his scent and the small excited sniffings and snufflings as he thrust his muzzle deep into tangles of old grass, searching for possible game.

Now and again there would be the sound of sudden movement as the coyote leaped high in the air to snap at a flying grasshopper, or pounced to pin an unlucky mouse under his paws. But both sounds and scent grew gradually fainter as he finished his business on the flat and finally disappeared into a shallow gully on the other side.

As the heat of the day increased, the Horse too moved off the flat, working his way slowly up the slope of the ridge ahead. On top an updraft made a little breeze strong enough to keep the biting flies away. And there the Horse settled down to rest and doze the afternoon away.

The sun was only a couple of hours high in the west when he stirred again. The small afternoon wind had sprung up and carried with it the faint smell of water. Facing in that direction, the Blind Horse left the ridge, crossed another shallow valley and the hogback of the far side of that. Coming onto a sagebrush flat, he moved more cautiously than before to avoid stumbling over the low tough bushes.

But he soon caught the warm smell of range cattle and dust from a deep stock path winding

through the sage. Turning into that, he found the going easier, and the smell of water grew stronger. When he came at last to the water hole, the cattle had already finished drinking, and he could smell and hear them grazing some way off.

Sniffing his way carefully across the wide band of trampled mud around the edges of the small pond, he drank, then moved off in the opposite direction from the grazing cattle. A colder wind was beginning to blow in fitful gusts, and there was the smell of rain in the air. Moving with the wind behind him, the Horse worked his way out of the sagebrush and up a shallow draw until a small thicket of box elder trees and plum bushes blocked his way. These and the sides of the draw offered him some protection from both wind and rain, so he settled down for the night.

For several days the Blind Horse drifted steadily but without hurry across the range. And in spite of his blindness, he seemed to have no difficulty in finding good grass or the location of the widely scattered water holes.

As he grazed, he sometimes caught the scent of fresh horse tracks in the grass, and one afternoon he came close to a small band of range horses. But even though he stayed in their neighborhood for several days, following them at a distance on their daily trips to water, he was never allowed to join them.

So it happened that one morning he was grazing some distance from a water hole where the band was drinking, when he heard men's voices and the creak of saddle leathers from a ridge behind him.

Throwing up his head and facing in the direction of the sounds, he snorted. Then, catching the scent of the men themselves, he wheeled away and broke into a run.

In his panic he ran directly toward the water hole and, before he realized his danger, he had stumbled and fallen to his knees in the treacherous mud. Struggling to his feet, the Blind Horse lunged and splashed his way through the mud and water and onto the dry ground on the other

side. But now he was in the middle of the milling band of range horses, crashing heavily against first one and then another.

By that time the riders were close behind and on either side of the confused horses, shouting and swinging long rope ends to drive the band ahead of them. Each time the Blind Horse tried to turn aside, a whistling rope or a horse and rider blocked his way. So there was nothing for him to do but run blindly with the rest. As they turned this way or that to avoid washouts or other obstacles, he was carried along by the press of horses on either side. He stumbled over sagebrush or little gullies from time to time, but luckily he did not fall.

After the first wild rush, the horses, guided by the riders on either side and pushed on by the ones behind, were allowed to settle down to an easy trot. For a while the men drove them straight across country, but after a few miles they were turned onto a wide stock trail that wound up an easy slope to a ridge above. At the top, the

path led through the wide opening between a pair of wing fences fanning out from the gate of a stout pole corral some distance down the slope. Seeing the fences, the horses in the lead tried to turn back but the ones behind, driven by the shouting riders, forced them ahead and through the gate.

As soon as they were all inside, the heavy gate was shut and the men went away. For a while the horses milled aimlessly about, looking for a way out. But the fence had no weak spots, and gradually they settled down to uneasy waiting.

Some of the bolder ones, overcoming their fear of the clanking windmill, even went cautiously to the water trough to drink. But the Blind Horse backed into a corner of the corral and stood there trembling, his coat darkened in great patches by nervous sweat.

2
The
Boy

THE Boy was already at the ranch when the Blind Horse was brought in with the others off the range.

He had appeared there sometime in the early spring, as nearly as anyone now remembers, with the old Buggy Salesman. The old man would start out from the railroad driving a good team hitched to a new buggy, and with two or three more of various styles hitched on behind in trailer fashion. He'd travel from town to town and ranch to ranch, peddling his buggies as others peddled extracts, cough cures, needles, or liniment.

But as is the case even with automobile dealers today, his dealings were not always for cash. He not only took old buggies and even old sets of harness in place of money, but often traded for horses as well. An old buggy could be hitched on behind the remaining new ones, and one or two extra horses could be tied alongside the team he was driving. But, as his second-hand horse herd grew, he would hire someone to drive them along behind.

The Boy had drifted into the old man's camp one morning, somewhere the other side of Miles City, Montana, and had been earning his keep by wrangling the little bunch of loose horses, washing road dust off the new buggies before they were shown to prospective customers, and helping with camp chores. The Buggy Salesman had no idea where he came from or what his name was—he simply called him Boy.

He wasn't much to look at, and it was hard to

judge his age. He might have been a big ten-
year-old or a small fifteen for all anyone could
tell. He wore a battered Stetson, well past its best
years and obviously a hand-me-down from
some long gone Texan. His boots, too, were Fort
Worths well along into advanced age—and big
enough that he'd be able to grow into them for
some years yet without danger of their pinching
his feet. The saddle on the potbellied old horse
he seemed to own had been made in Miles City
years before the Boy was born. His mismatched
spurs, too, were Montana style—short iron
shanks and sharp rowells the size of dimes instead of the long goosenecks and "dollar rowels"
of the southern ranges. So to judge his origins
from his gear was impossible.

During his layover at the ranch, the old man
sold all his loose horses to a passing trader and no
longer needed a wrangler. So when he left, the
Boy stayed on as a sort of chore boy.

At first the Ranch Owner and the men around
the ranch thought it was strange that, while he

didn't appear to be sullen by nature, he never answered when spoken to. But the old Buggy Salesman explained that, while the Boy could hear and understand what was said to him, for some reason or other he was unable to speak. He could make some sounds, but nothing more.

However, he seemed to understand animals and birds, and in some fashion was able to communicate with them. When he first came to the ranch, he had a tame magpie that he talked to in a strange wordless fashion that the bird seemed to understand.

Later he found a nest of baby rabbits whose mother had probably been taken by a coyote or hawk. He put them in a box filled with rags and fed them diluted condensed milk with a medicine dropper until they were big enough to forage for themselves. As they got older, they followed him about as he did the ranch chores and, for some reason, neither the cats nor the ranch dogs ever bothered them.

The coyote pup a passing cowboy had given

him later also became a familiar sight around the ranch, following the Boy and the young rabbits. And the day old Ring, the one-eyed vicious-tempered ranch dog, tangled with a porcupine, he lay without a snarl or whimper while the Boy removed the painful quills one by one from his cheeks and muzzle.

But whoever he was and wherever he came from, the Boy was a good worker. He wrangled the saddle horses, chopped and carried wood, hauled water, and did the hundred-and-one small jobs that have to be done around any ranch. And after a while, nobody paid attention to the fact he could not speak.

3
The
Horse-
Breaker

WHEN the Ranch Owner and the Cowboy, who spent his spare time breaking new horses to fill out the remuda, walked down to look over the wild ones that had just been brought in, the Boy and his animals followed close behind them.

Sitting on the top rail of the corral, the two men watched the horses milling around below, judging their tempers, looks, and condition. When they agreed on one that would possibly make a good saddle horse, it was separated from the others and run into another pen by the men down on the ground.

They had picked out several before the Horse-breaker pointed to the Blind Horse still standing alone in the corner of the corral.

"What about the mouse-colored one with the dark patch on his face?" he asked.

"He doesn't look like one of ours," the Ranch Owner told him. "He must be a stray."

"I've looked at him on both sides," one of the cowboys told him, "and he doesn't have a brand on him anywhere."

Any animal on the range that carries no own-er's brand belongs to whoever picks him up and, after carefully looking the stray over again, the Ranch Owner said, "All right, run him into the pen with the others. If he turns out all right, and nobody comes looking for him, we'll brand him later."

And as he climbed down from the fence he spoke again. "Turn the rest loose and run them

back out onto the range," he said. And he and the Horsebreaker walked away.

Right after breakfast next morning, the Horsebreaker had one of the new horses run into the round roping corral for its first lesson. After the gate was closed, he stood for a while by the scarred snubbing post in the center, quietly talking to the horse as it circled the corral looking for a way out. Making no sudden moves, the man slowly rolled and lit a cigarette while he waited for the horse's first panic to pass.

Then, moving away from the post with the coil of his rope in his left hand and trailing the opened noose from his right, he waited for the horse to pass him. With a sharp side-arm swing, he flipped the loop neatly over the animal's head and twitched it snug around its neck.

The horse, feeling the rope tighten, snorted and reared high onto his hind legs, then lunged away. But by taking a couple of turns of the rope around the post, the Horsebreaker easily stopped the horse's rush, slowly taking up the rope's

slack to bring him closer and closer to the snubbing post.

Most horses quickly learn that fighting the rope only draws the choking noose tighter. So this one was soon standing braced at the end of the rope, breathing heavily while the Horsebreaker talked softly to him. When the man moved, the horse would snort and lunge again, but each time the struggle was shorter, until at last he stood quietly while the man undid the turns of his rope from the snubbing post, flipped the noose free from the horse's head, and turned him loose for the day, his first lesson finished.

One after another, the Horsebreaker dealt with several more of the wild horses as he had the first and, as soon as they stopped fighting the rope, he turned them loose.

And then the mouse-colored Stray, in his turn, was run through the gate. When he smelled the man, he did as the others had done, and whirled toward the fence. But instead of turning to fol-

low it around the circle, he crashed straight into it, then reared in a frantic attempt to climb over. Falling back, he scrambled to his feet and again crashed headlong into the fence.

When the Horse showed no sign of giving up his attempts to crash through or climb over the fence, the Horsebreaker at last cast his loop over his head and twitched it snug. As he felt the noose tighten around his neck, the Horse made a hoarse bawling sound and reared high on his hind legs. The rope around the snubbing post held fast, however, and the Horse crashed heavily onto his back. When he'd gotten to his feet again, he faced the man, braced himself, and pulled backwards until his neck was stretched to what looked like the breaking point.

With his weight against the rope pulling the choking noose tighter and tighter against his windpipe, the Horse stood braced with his nostrils distended and his tongue showing between his half-opened jaws. He breathed in great, hoarse, rasping sobs that gradually became

weaker until at last he went slowly to his knees.

Seeing the Horse weaken, the man by the post loosened the rope a little. With the pressure of the noose gone, the Horse drew in a few great whistling breaths, then struggled to his feet and again threw himself backwards against the rope.

And again, when the tightening noose choked him to his knees, the man gave him slack.

Time after time the struggle was repeated. The Stray's coat was black with sweat and his tongue, when it showed, was smeared with corral dirt, but still he showed no sign of giving up.

The Boy had been watching through the fence since the Horse had been brought into the corral with the Horsebreaker, and now a cowboy and the Ranch Owner, on the way to the ranch house for dinner, stopped by also.

The Horse was on his knees again, so the Horsebreaker gave him a little slack in the rope and turned to where the others sat on the fence.

"This is the worst spooked horse I ever worked with," he said, wiping sweat from his

face. "I'd guess somebody has abused him badly some time or other. He's got scars round his head as if he'd been beaten with a chain or some such thing.

"He's pure outlaw now," the Horsebreaker went on. "He fights the rope 'til he chokes himself down, then as soon as I give him a little air, he gets up and starts all over. And before I got the rope on him, he almost managed to climb the fence. He just isn't going to give up."

"Too bad," the Ranch Owner said. "He's a right likely looking horse."

By now the Horse, still breathing in great gasps, was struggling back to his feet, and the Horse-breaker spoke again.

"How about coming in here and hog-tying him for me when he chokes down this time?" he asked. "I want to look at him close before I turn him loose for good."

So when the Horse went to his knees, the Horsebreaker left the rope tight while the others

quickly tied his feet together and gently pushed him onto his side, where he lay helpless.

The Horsebreaker loosened the noose from the Horse's neck, then spent some time examining his head and muzzle. Getting to his feet he said, "Besides being outlaw, that Horse is blind."

"Blind?" the Ranch Owner asked. "You sure?"

"Yep," the Horsebreaker told him. "I'd begun to suspect it from the way he acted, and just now I looked real careful. He's blind as a bat."

For a little while, the men stood watching the Horse as he struggled weakly against the ropes around his feet.

"It's too bad," the Ranch Owner finally said. "But it doesn't seem right to turn him back on the range, him being blind. Maybe we ought to shoot him?"

The Ranch Owner felt a touch on his arm and turned to find the Boy beside him. Pointing at the Horse and then to himself, he seemed to be trying to say something.

"What's he trying to say, do you reckon?" the Ranch Owner asked.

"I think he wants the Stray," the Horsebreaker said. "You know how he is about animals."

"You think you could tame that Horse, is that it?" the Ranch Owner asked the Boy, who nodded his head.

For a while longer, the men stood there without saying anything, while the Boy anxiously watched both the Horse and their faces. They looked at the Boy, at the tame magpie on his shoulder, and at the half-grown coyote lying on the ground with the young rabbits.

After a bit the Horsebreaker nodded and, half to himself, he said, "You know, he just might do it."

The Ranch Owner thought for a while longer, then turned to the Boy and said, "Spooked like that Horse is, I don't see how even you could break him. And even if you did, what good would a blind horse be to anybody? He's too big to keep just for a pet like your other animals."

The Boy made no answer, simply stood there making soft noises to himself and the Horse lying hog-tied on the ground. After a while, the Ranch Owner spoke again.

"All right," he said to the Horsebreaker, "let the Horse up and put him in one of the corrals by himself."

And turning to the Boy, he went on, "If you think you can gentle that Blind Outlaw in your spare time, he's yours. And the day you can ride him up to the house, I'll give you a bill of sale for him."

4
Boy
and
Horse

So THE Blind Horse was separated from the others—and put into an unused corral by himself. The Boy still had his chores to do, but nonetheless he found dozens of excuses to go by just to look at the Horse, or to see that the water trough was full.

After supper he came back, with his small animals following, and brought hay from the stack yard to put by the water trough. Then, climbing to the top rail of the corral fence, he sat

for a long time, whittling on a stick, while crooning and chirping in his soft wordless way to the Horse or to the magpie perched on the post nearby.

Across the corral, the Blind Horse stood backed into a corner, shifting his feet nervously as he faced the place where the Boy sat. Now and again he cleared his nostrils with a soft snorting sound as he delicately sniffed the air to sort out the strange scents of the Boy, the young coyote, and the small rabbits.

He flung up his head and pointed his ears at each unfamiliar ranch sound—the squeal of a horse from the nearby pasture, the slam of a screen door, or the sounds of voices from the bunkhouse. But after a time, when the Boy made no move to leave his perch on the fence, the Horse seemed to relax a little. He occasionally switched his long burr-matted tail or stamped a foot to dislodge a fly. But his sharp pointed ears were always set to catch the Boy's soft voice as it went on and on, sounding strangely like some small bird talking to itself.

When the dusk had thickened until the Boy could see the Horse only as a light-colored blur against the fence, he climbed quietly down the outside of the corral. With his animals following him, he went back to the bunkhouse, and the Horse was left alone.

During the next few days the Horsebreaker and the other cowboys used any handy excuse to go by the corral, hoping to see how the Boy who couldn't speak would go about taming the Blind Outlaw. But as far as they could tell, he was in no hurry to begin, and there was no way they could ask what his plan was.

Each morning he brought more hay and made sure the water trough was full. And he went through the corral a dozen times a day, on one errand or another, simply coming in one gate and going out the other without stopping or making any move toward the Horse.

The Horse, whenever he heard the Boy's footsteps and caught his scent, would back into the far corner and stand with his head high, nostrils wide and ears flicking forward and back as he listened for the creak of the opening gate. And as the small procession passed him, he turned his head, sniffing and listening to follow their progress. But when they seemed intent on some business of their own, he made no other move.

For several days this went on—the Boy making his trips through the Blind Horse's corral at odd times during the day, and sitting on the top rail from suppertime until dark. The Horse still stayed watchfully in his corner whenever the Boy and the animals were about, but as the days went on he showed less and less sign of nervousness.

Then one night after supper the Boy brought his old saddle horse from where he'd been grazing in the little horse pasture and turned him loose in the corral. The old horse walked over to the Blind One in the corner and, stretching his neck far out, touched noses with him to get his scent. Then he went to the water trough for a drink before picking over the hay on the ground.

Later the Boy went to the bunkhouse and

brought back his bedroll and pushed it between the lower bars before climbing to his usual perch on the top rail. There the Boy made his wordless sounds to the horses and the small animals while he busily braided narrow strips cut from soft boot leather to make one of the quirts he sold to passing cowboys. The Blind Horse, from his corner, divided his attention between the Boy's voice and the movements of the old saddle horse.

The Blind Horse in his corner spent the night awake, stirring nervously at the slightest sound from where the Boy and the small animals slept. At first daylight the Boy got up and rolled his bed, placing it neatly beside the fence before going to the water trough to wash. While he was doing these things, he made his usual wordless sounds to himself, but seemed to pay no attention to the Blind Horse, and when he was finished he led the old horse, with the small animals following, out through the gate.

From then on the Boy not only made his usual trips through the corral during the day, but spent

every night there as well. While he worked quietly at his leatherwork before bedtime, the soft conversational sounds that were not words went on and on. The small animals, going about their own affairs, often passed close to the Blind Horse's feet. The Horse heard the sounds they made and recognized, without alarm, their warm furry smells. But he threw up his head with ears sharply forward at any sound of movement from where the Boy sat on the fence.

For some days the Horse backed into his corner whenever the Boy and his animals appeared. But before long he began to cock his ears forward in interested fashion as he followed the sounds of the little processions through his corral, or listened to the sound of the Boy's voice in the evenings. He still remained watchful, starting at any strange sound, but before long he began to move freely around the corral in the nights after the Boy had gone to bed. Often he followed the older horse as he searched under the bottom rail of the fence for odd tufts of grass. And now he spent much of every night dozing on his feet, waking only when he heard the Boy stir in his sleep. During the day he sometimes cautiously approached the bedroll beside the corral fence, nuzzling it lightly as he sniffed the now familiar scent of the Boy.

And evenings, when the Boy brought the old saddle horse into the corral for the night, the Blind Outlaw, instead of backing into his corner, now often stood quietly a little distance off. He'd seem to listen interestedly to the Boy's voice and the small sounds as he took off the old horse's halter and neatly coiled the lead rope.

Then one night the Boy, while scratching and petting the old horse, took three or four carrots from his pocket and fed them to him one by one. Hearing the crisp crunching sounds as the old horse ate them, the Blind One suddenly stretched his head forward, ears flicking and his nostrils wide. Snuffling softly, trying to catch the faint scent of the carrots, he cautiously shifted his feet this way and that but without coming any closer. Still listening and testing the air, he waited where

he was until the Boy had gone back to his place
on the top rail. Then cautiously, a short step at a
time, turning his head often to listen for any
movement from the Boy, he went to where the
old horse stood and snuffled in the dust, searching out tiny bits the other had dropped.

A range-raised horse usually pays no attention
to carrots, apples, and such things, so now the
Boy was sure that before he turned outlaw this
one had been someone's pet, accustomed to being fed tidbits of one kind and another.

From then on the Boy brought some treat
from the garden or the kitchen each night. And
while the other crunched the crisp bits, the Blind
One listened and snuffed the air as before. And
each night he came a little closer, but always
poised to back away at any unusual sound of
movement.

So far the Boy had seemed to ignore the Blind
Horse. But one night when, keeping the old
horse between them, he had come closer than
usual, the Boy quietly flipped a carrot out in his

direction. At the sound the Horse whirled away and stood snorting softly some distance off.

But later, while the Boy went on feeding other bits to the old horse, the Blind One cautiously sniffed his way to where the carrot had dropped and picked it up. Stepping back, he stood crunching it until it was gone, then sniffed about in the dust for more.

Each night after that the Blind Horse came a little closer, but always kept the old horse between himself and the Boy. And when he heard the treat drop in front of him, he'd reach down without hesitation and pick it up.

Then one night the Boy took a piece of dried apple from his pocket but, instead of tossing it to the Horse as he had been doing, he simply reached under the old horse's neck and held it toward the other.

The Horse stretched his neck forward, blowing softly through his nostrils as he caught the sweet apple scent. He stamped, shifting his feet one way and another, coming a few inches closer, then backing off, but stayed out of reach.

So after a bit the Boy fed the piece to the old horse and climbed with his leatherwork to his usual place on the top rail.

While he watched, the Horse sniffed about for the treat he'd expected to find on the ground, then went to search out the tiny scraps the old horse had dropped.

The next night and the one after that, the Horse stood nervously nearby, sniffing and tossing his head while the old horse was fed all the small bits the Boy had brought. But the third night, his greed finally overcame his caution. This time, when the Boy reached past the old horse, holding out a piece of jelly bread, the Horse inched toward him and gently took it from his fingers before stepping back out of reach.

When the Horse had finished the bread, the Boy coaxed him back to take a piece of dried apple and, later, some bits of dried apricot from his hand. But still he would not come close enough to be touched, staying always on the far side of the older horse.

5
Brush
and
Currycomb

SOMETIMES the Boy would be away from the ranch from morning until night, helping repair fences, greasing windmills, or cleaning out springs. During those days the Blind Horse would move restlessly around his corral, often going over to sniff at the Boy's bedroll by the fence, or standing at the gate with his ears cocked in the direction of the bunkhouse.

And when the Boy came in after supper, bringing the old horse with him, the Blind Horse

44

would come part way across the corral to meet them. Stopping a little way off, he'd stand flicking his ears and listening to the sounds of the saddle being taken off, or sniffing at the small animals as they came past him. And when he heard the rustling as the Boy reached in his pockets for the things he'd brought from the kitchen, he'd cautiously move closer. Every night he took his share from the Boy's fingers, but only when the old horse stood between them. He still wouldn't let himself be touched and, at all other times, kept his distance.

Then one rainy night, the Boy spread his bedroll in the shed at the end of the corral, where the older horse had already taken shelter. Before he went to sleep, he saw the Blind Horse standing out in his usual place, seeming not to mind the light drizzle. But in the night, wakened by the feel of a warm breath on his face, he looked up without moving and found the Outlaw standing over him in the dark, gently sniffing his face, hair, and bedding. In the morning, however, the Horse was back in his usual place.

From then on, whenever the Boy went through the Horse's corral in the daytime, he gave his soft birdlike call before he reached the gate but, instead of going straight on through, as he had been doing, now he would stop for a bit just inside. Clucking and chirping to the Horse, he'd take a cold biscuit or a bit of dried apple out of his pocket and hold it out.

As long as the Boy made no move to come close, the Horse would stand quietly, his neck stretched forward, trying to catch the scent of what it was the Boy was holding in his hand. Sometimes he'd shift his feet a little, blowing softly but, without the other horse there, he would not come close.

The Boy would carry on this odd, one-sided, wordless conversation for a while, then carefully toss the treat toward the Horse's feet before making some signal to the small animals lolling in the dust nearby and leading them out through the other gate.

The Horse would wait until he heard the far

gate close, then step forward to sniff out whatever the Boy had dropped on the ground. But he was losing much of his distrust and, in the evenings, with the old horse between them, he was taking tidbits from the Boy's hand with less and less caution. And he was becoming more and more greedy for the little snacks.

So now even without the old horse there, the Boy was able to coax him a little closer each day until at last he'd not only take the things from the Boy's fingers, but would nuzzle and nibble at his pockets when they were being doled out too slowly. And the day the Boy first reached up and lightly scratched him behind the ears, he seemed not to notice.

From then on the strange relationship between the Boy and the Blind Outlaw developed rapidly. Whenever he heard the Boy coming toward the corral, the Horse would nicker softly and trot to the gate to meet him. After giving out whatever bits he'd brought, the Boy would stand for a while rubbing the Horse's forehead and

stroking the velvety muzzle, the familiar sound of his soft voice going on and on.

The Horse seemed to listen intently to the Boy's voice, flicking his ears backwards and forward. And when he walked away, the Horse would follow close behind, often nudging his back or shoulder in friendly fashion with his muzzle.

Sometimes after supper, the Ranch Owner and the Horsebreaker came down to sit a while on the top rail, talking quietly to each other while they watched the Boy and the Horse below. If he was alone in the corral, the first sound or scent of the men would send the Blind Horse to his place in the far corner, where he would stand, snorting and nervously shifting his feet. But with the Boy there, he seemed less fearful. And as long as they stayed quiet on the fence, seeming not to threaten him, he gradually came to ignore them.

One such night, the men found the Boy and the Horse playing what seemed to be a strange game of follow-the-leader. While they watched, the

Boy scratched and stroked the Horse's head for a while, then, after making a curious chirping signal, he turned and walked away while the Horse stood where he was, with his ears cocked sharply forward.

After taking a few steps, the Boy stopped, turned, and chirped again. The Horse, when he heard the small sound, walked forward and stopped directly in front of the Boy, rubbing his forehead against his chest and nibbling gently at his shirt. After another soft chirping sound to the Horse, the Boy walked off in another direction and, this time, the Horse walked beside him.

For some time the men watched as the Boy and the Horse walked this way and that—starting, stopping, turning to one side or the other. What the various chirping sounds meant, only the Boy and the Blind Horse knew. But the Horse seemed to understand them and, without being touched, he followed the Boy closely as if he'd been on a lead rope.

"A strange thing," the Horsebreaker remarked

after a while. "The Horse can't see, and neither one can talk, yet they seem really to understand each other."

"Yeah," the Ranch Owner agreed. "And I'd have been willing to bet that the Boy would never be able to get a hand on that Horse, spooked like he was."

They watched a while longer, then climbed down the outside of the fence and went away.

One evening the Boy brought the old horse into the corral with his saddle still on. While the Blind Horse nuzzled his hands and sniffed at his pockets, the boy started taking the saddle off. At the first rattle of the loosened cinch buckle, the Blind Horse snorted and backed away. The Boy paid no attention, but went on making some unnecessary adjustments to the stirrup leathers before pulling the saddle off and dragging it to the fence.

But after a few nights, he began to lose his fear of the sounds and, before long, would stand unconcernedly sniffing the Boy's pockets all the while he was dealing with the saddle. Even when the dragging cinch brushed his leg one night, he paid it no attention.

And now when the Boy climbed to his place on the top rail to work a while at his leather braiding, the Horse would come to stand close by the fence just below him. And instead of spending the nights at the far side of the corral, he now slept, standing, close by the Boy's bed.

The Blind Horse hadn't completely shed his rough winter coat, and the ragged patches of long winter hair mixed with dirt and dried mud gave him a scruffy, unkempt look. So one evening the Boy brought an old curry comb and brush into the corral and let the Horse smell them after he'd eaten the pieces of jelly bread he'd brought from the house. After he had carefully sniffed and nibbled at the tools, the Horse let the Boy begin lightly brushing the side of his jaw and his forehead.

That first evening the Boy worked gently, brushing only the Horse's head and the sides of his neck. When the brush or the currycomb pulled hairs out, along with patches of dried

mud, the Horse would flinch or reach around to nibble at the Boy's hands. But by the time his head and neck had been brushed until they were sleek and shiny, he seemed to be enjoying the attention.

When he'd done that much, the Boy cleaned the currycomb and brush, fed the Horse a piece of brown sugar, and climbed to the top of the fence to work a while at his leather braiding.

But each night, he spent some time on the grooming, standing on a box to reach the Horse's back and rump. Even the gentlest horse will object to the touch of the brush on his flanks and legs but, as the Blind Horse became more and more accustomed to the feel of the Boy's hands on his skin, those places, too, were brushed and curried.

It was some time, however, before he would let his feet be picked up and examined without snorting and backing away. But the Boy continued his coaxing and chirping and, in the end, the Horse stood without objection even when the Boy took a hoof between his knees and started

smoothing and trimming the rough broken edges with an old rasp.

By now the Blind Horse had begun to take on a smooth, well-groomed look. But his long mane and tail, matted with mud and cockleburs, still had to be dealt with. So one night instead of using the brush, the Boy took his pocketknife and, standing on the box, started pulling and cutting away the tangles in the Horse's forelock.

With no rope or halter to hold him, the Horse was free to back out of reach at any time. But though he sometimes stamped a foot, or swung his head to nibble gently at the Boy's shirt or hands as the knife was tugged through an unusually tough tangle, he seemed not to object to the trimming.

Night after night, the little pile of coarse horse hair by the fence grew larger as the Blind Horse lost his ragged range horse appearance. And by the time the Boy had finished, the Outlaw was as neatly trimmed and groomed as any saddle horse on the ranch.

6
The
Horse
Escapes

A DAY or two after he'd finished grooming and trimming the Horse, the Boy was feeding him some dried apricots he'd taken from the kitchen after dinner when he looked up and saw a tall, yellow-gray column of smoke boiling up from beyond the ridge to the south.

For weeks the weather had been hot, dry, and windy—and prairie fires in ranch country were even more feared than tornadoes. One running out of control might destroy thousands of acres of grass as well as buildings in its path. So at the first sign of smoke, men from all parts of the range dropped whatever they were doing and rode out to fight the dreaded flames.

On most ranches and homesteads, the buildings were protected by a wide fireguard—a strip of plowed ground that, ordinarily, the creeping flames could not cross. But even so, there was always danger that blowing sparks and brands might set new fires inside the protected islands. So when the men had gone, the women and children left behind filled water barrels, washtubs, and buckets, and put wet sacks, rakes, and hoes in handy places. Fighting fire, in that country, was everybody's business.

So within minutes after the Boy had given the alarm, everyone on the ranch was busy. The team was quickly hitched to the wagon, while water barrels were loaded, along with shovels, pieces of canvas, and old grain sacks. As soon as those things had been done, and the water bar-

rels filled at the windmill, the Ranch Owner drove the wagon out the gate, followed by the others on their horses.

With the fire moving away from the ranch, nobody needed to stay behind, so the Boy, on his potbellied old horse, rode with them. The Blind Horse had been standing at the corral gate, poking his muzzle between the planks, sniffing the air and listening to the unfamiliar sounds. And as the Boy rode away, he nickered softly, but got no answer.

After several miles they came in sight of the fire, already burning in a great arc a mile or more across, leaving behind it a broad band of blackened, smoking ground. On the dry flats where the grass was short, the flames crept slowly but steadily ahead but, in the swales and occasional patches of high grass, they roared up to great heights, into boiling clouds of greasy black smoke. Sparks and burning brands, picked up by the wind, swirled high in the air, then fell to the ground, starting new blazes in the unburned grass ahead.

The men quickly unhitched the team, well upwind from the burned ground, and tied them and the saddle horses to the wheels. Then after wetting their neckerchiefs and tying them over their noses, they moved to the line of fire, beating at the flames with pieces of canvas and sacks they'd soaked in the water barrels.

Following them, others worked with rakes and shovels to cover the smoldering spots before they could break into flame again.

Two riders from another ranch were already riding their snorting, protesting horses at a gallop along the line of fire, dragging a water-soaked tarpaulin over the flames by ropes tied to their saddle horns.

Little by little the advancing line was broken into smaller sections, somewhat reducing the intense heat. As men on foot moved into these gaps with their sacks and shovels, others went on to smother and beat out the scattered fires set by blowing sparks.

It was hot, dirty work, with the thick acrid smoke making the eyes smart and breathing dif-

ficult. Flying ash and sparks burned holes in men's clothing and raised small blisters on their skin.

But as more and more men arrived from the more distant ranches, the fire was gradually brought under control. By late afternoon the last of advancing flames had been beaten down, and the newcomers moved back and forth over the blackened ground, shoveling dirt on smoldering sagebrush roots and the occasional small islands of still burning grass.

These latecomers would stay until the wind went down in the evening, making sure no hidden spark was fanned into flame again. So at last the men from the ranch shouldered their tools and started the long walk back to where they'd left the wagon and horses. On the way, a man from a ranch farther to the north joined them. He'd arrived late and left his horse tied to their wagon. Beyond saying a courteous "Howdy," they were all too tired for talk.

It wasn't until they had thrown their shovels

and tattered sacks into the wagon and were standing about pouring water over their heads and checking their blisters, that the Stranger spoke up.

"I'm sorry," he told the Ranch Owner, "but I accidentally let a horse out of your corral when I came through."

"Probably one of the old workhorses," the Ranch Owner answered. "He'll be hanging around when we get back."

"I dunno," the Rider said. "He was plenty spooked.

"I came down the trail between your wing fences," he went on. "Didn't seem to be any horses in the corrals, and I was in a hurry, so I left the big gate open, and the one into the next corral, too. I was just about to open the gate on the far side when this horse I hadn't seen busted out through the gate behind me. For some reason or other, he missed the far gate and crashed straight into the fence instead. Then he tried to climb over and fell back. While he was down I

shook down my rope and, as he got up that time, I dabbed a loop over his head to keep him from getting out the gate.

"But when that rope tightened on him, he went plumb loco! Before I could dally my end of it around the saddle horn, he'd jerked it out of my hands and taken off, straight through your big gate. The last I saw of him, he was heading for the ridge, dragging my best rope with him."

For a while nobody said anything. Then after looking at the Boy, who had made a sudden sound, the Ranch Owner spoke up.

"Wasn't your fault," he said to the Rider. "That Horse is blind, and an outlaw to boot. He goes crazy at the touch of a rope."

"I couldn't do anything with him," the Horse-breaker remarked. "Lately the Boy here has been working him in his spare time, trying to gentle him."

"I'm really sorry," the Rider said. "But I'll be glad to help you get him back."

"It's really the Boy's Horse," the Ranch Owner

answered. "He'll probably have better luck catching him than any of us would. But thanks, anyway."

Then turning to the silent Boy, who looked close to tears, he went on. "When we get back to the ranch, you leave your chores. We'll take care of them. You go on and look for the Horse if you want."

After that nothing more was said and, after hitching the team to the wagon, the tired men mounted their horses for the long ride back to the ranch.

7
The
Search

It was almost suppertime when the Boy and the rest of the men rode over the last ridge and down through the ranch yard gate. While the horses were being unhitched from the wagon, the Boy went to the kitchen and quickly made himself a sandwich and put some dried apples in his pocket for the Blind Horse, in case he found him.

Then after watering the old horse at the windmill, he rode out to start his search. The Stranger offered again to help him, but the Boy only raised a hand and shook his head.

He had no trouble following the Horse's tracks and the mark of the trailing rope in the deep dust of the wide stock path to the top of the ridge. But just over the top, the path swung sharply to the left to avoid a deep gully, and the tracks showed that the Horse, instead of turning to follow it, had plunged straight ahead and over the bank.

Sorting out the signs in the torn-up dirt in the bottom of the washout, the Boy found where the Horse had rolled, struggled to his feet again, and scrambled up the farther bank. But after that the tracks disappeared in the grass and there was no way of telling which way he had gone.

So the Boy rode on, stopping at the top of every ridge to look around. Twice he saw lone horses in the distance, but both were grazing quietly so he didn't bother to go closer. He was sure that even after the Horse's first panic had passed, he would still be trying to get away from the trailing rope.

The sun went down and, before long, the deepening dusk made more search impossible,

so at last he turned back toward the ranch.

The next morning the Boy was up at daybreak to do his chores before riding out to continue his search. Starting again at the place where the Horse had climbed the bank of the washout, he rode back and forth in wider and wider arcs, examining each dusty stock path and every patch of bare ground for some sign that would tell him which way the Horse had run.

Now and again he found a hoofprint or two and once a patch of trampled ground and a fresh hole where a clump of sage had been pulled up by the roots. It looked to the Boy as if the Horse's trailing rope had become entangled in the bush, and he'd struggled for some time before managing to pull free.

But these small signs were of little help, for the Horse seemed to still be running only to escape the dragging rope, veering off in a new direction each time it touched his legs or caught for a moment on bushes or clumps of high grass.

So there was nothing the Boy could do but ride

at random, stopping on the top of every ridge or small hill to look about. He looked into any gully or washout big enough to hide a fallen horse, and carefully read the tracks in the mud around each spring and water hole.

There were small thickets of wild plum and box elder in almost every draw and, if the Blind Horse had blundered into one of these, he might easily have gotten entangled and be unable to escape. So the Boy looked carefully into those places also.

But although he rode until after sundown before turning back toward the ranch, he had still found no sign to tell him which way the Horse had gone.

It was near noon the next day when the Boy, searching the rocky country at the head of Cedar Creek, found a few faint hoofprints in patches of soft ground in the bottom of a little draw leading up to the rimrock above.

There was no way the Boy could be sure that the tracks had been made by the Blind Horse,

and the draw appeared to end at the base of the rock cliffs above. But as nearly as he could tell the tracks led upwards, so, walking and leading his old horse, he followed them.

The head of the draw was partly blocked by a thicket of wild plum and choke cherry, but an old stock path led through it and around a rocky outcropping that concealed the entrance to a little box canyon. Except for the gap where the Boy now stood, the floor of the place was surrounded on all sides by overhanging rocky cliffs. Thick grass grew on the level ground, and water seeped from a little spring under the rocks at one side.

Backed against the rocky wall beyond the spring stood the Blind Horse.

The rope was still around his neck, and his hide was smeared with mud, and skinned and scratched in places. But otherwise he seemed unharmed. He had heard the old horse and the Boy coming along the stock path, and now he shifted his feet, snorting and snuffing softly, but made no other move.

For a bit the Boy simply stood where he was, talking softly to the Horse in his wordless way. At the sound of the Boy's voice, the Blind Horse stretched his neck far forward, cocking his ears and widening his nostrils, listening and delicately testing the air for the familiar scent. When the Boy still made no move toward him, the Horse took a short, hesitant step forward, then stopped. It was plain that he was still badly spooked from his experience with the rope, and still fearful even though he seemed to recognize the Boy's scent and voice.

The Boy, moving quietly and without hurry, turned to the old horse, took off the saddle, and turned him loose. After shaking himself, the Horse walked toward the Blind One, touched muzzles with him, then started cropping the green grass growing around the spring.

After putting the saddle neatly down, the Boy squatted on his heels, his back against a rock, chirping and crooning to himself while he thought about what to do next.

The young coyote, who had been lying under

a bush, panting, got to his feet and began to explore. As he sniffed inquisitively under the scraggly bushes or poked his sharp nose into the grass tussocks and small holes in the rocks, the Horse started, then listened attentively to the little rustlings and snufflings, but showed no sign of alarm. And when the pup came to where he stood and sniffed daintily at his forefeet, the Horse dropped his head and nuzzled the soft fur.

At any sound of movement from the Boy's direction, the Horse threw up his head and snorted softly. So the Boy continued to simply sit there against the rock, watching the Horse and making his soft reassuring sounds.

For a while the little box canyon was quiet except for the Boy's soft voice going on and on, and the small rustlings from where the young coyote went about his explorations among the rocks. Then the boy untied a package from the saddle beside him and began to eat his lunch.

At the first rattling of the paper bag, the Horse shifted his feet nervously and, turning his head from side to side, listened and sniffed for the meaning of the sound. But as the Boy went on with his eating, making coaxing sounds between bites, the Horse began moving toward him, a short cautious step at a time. Between steps he'd stop to listen, stretching his neck to catch the scent and sound of the Boy, then come slowly forward again. He held his head to one side to keep the rope away from his feet, but otherwise seemed not to be bothered by it.

As the Horse came closer, the Boy got quietly to his feet, chirping softly, and held out part of a brown-sugar sandwich. At the sound of his movement, the Horse stopped and backed up a step or two. But catching the sweet smell of the bread and sugar, he came slowly forward again until he could stretch his neck far enough to snatch it from the Boy's fingers.

Still making his soft chirping noises, the Boy took another piece of sandwich from the bag. But this one he held inside his closed fingers so that the Horse could not snatch it as he had done with the first. Still standing where he could reach

the Boy's hand only by stretching his neck to the utmost, he gently nuzzled the closed fingers with his soft lips, trying to get at the bread. When he was able to get only a few crumbs, he finally seemed to overcome his fear and stepped closer, impatiently nudging the Boy's arm with his muzzle.

Stepping back a little, the Boy chirped again and opened his hand. The Horse followed him without hesitation and took the bread. Then after nibbling and blowing his warm breath on the Boy's palm as he searched for the last sweet bits, he rubbed his forehead against the Boy's shirt and sniffed his pockets, looking for more.

Unhurriedly the Boy gave the Horse the last scraps of his lunch, rubbing his soft muzzle and ears between bits.

For a while the Boy made no move to take the rope from the Horse's neck, but when he tugged it lightly to see that the noose was not too tight, the Horse only tossed his head, then went on sniffing at the empty lunch bag. Gathering the dragging end of the rope into a loose coil, the Boy let the Horse smell it, then chirped to him and started walking away. The Horse followed him as he'd done in the corral at the ranch, rubbing his head against the Boy's shoulder as he walked.

For a while the Boy and the Horse moved this way and that inside the box canyon, starting, stopping, and turning as the Boy gave the little signals the Horse seemed to remember and understand. Later he carefully took the noose from around the Horse's neck and fastened the coil to his saddle. Then he caught and saddled the old horse and rode out of the canyon with the Blind Horse following close behind.

When they were out in the open, the Horse trotted a few steps to catch up, then walked close alongside the old horse, rubbing his head against the Boy's knee from time to time as they went without hurry toward the ranch.

8
The
Saddle
Horse

For the first few days back at the ranch, the Horse seemed nervous and uneasy when the Boy was out of sight. He'd start and fling his head up at any sudden sound or, if the Ranch Owner or any of the men came near the corral, he'd back into a corner and stand there trembling.

But when the Boy and the small animals appeared, he met them at the gate, rubbing his muzzle against the Boy's shirt and sniffing at his pockets. And he seemed to no longer object to the tickling of the magpie's sharp claws when the bird flew up to perch on his back.

The Horse had lost his well-groomed look, and the Boy spent several evenings standing on the box, brushing dried mud from his coat and pulling away the cockleburs and tangles in his mane and tail.

The Horse seemed to enjoy these sessions, cocking his ears back and forth, listening to the Boy's voice going on and on. When he felt the sharp sting of the salve being rubbed into the deep scratches and skinned places, he'd shift his feet and snort a little or reach around to nibble lightly at the Boy's hands or the back of his shirt, but that was all.

The young rabbits were nearly grown and had already moved into the high grass somewhere in the big pasture, but the small coyote and the magpie still followed the Boy as he went about his chores. And sometimes now, he opened the corral gate and let the Horse join the little procession.

In the corral there had been nothing for the Horse to avoid except the water trough and the fence itself. But in the yard there was the windmill and the big water tank as well as the woodpile, wagons, hayracks, and the mowing machine to be looked out for.

Although the Horse could easily tell where the windmill stood by listening for the squeak and rattle of the pump rods, the other things gave no warning and were more difficult to avoid. But after a few painful bumps, he learned to sniff them out, and followed the Boy without too much trouble.

For some time the Boy had been busy with his leather strings, braiding a fancy noseband and making a hackamore for the Horse and, one evening after supper, he put it on him. At the first touch of the leather around his muzzle, the Horse flung up his head to shake the thing off. But as the Boy went on making his coaxing sounds, he quickly quieted and stood still while the headstall was slipped over his ears, and the throat latch tied. No rope was fastened to the hackamore yet, but the Boy took a light hold on one of the cheek pieces and led the Horse this way and that for a while to get him accustomed to the feel.

The Horse was still uneasy when he heard or smelled the Ranch Owner or any of the cowboys who often came to see how the Boy was getting along with his Outlaw. As time went on, however, he paid less and less attention, even when they came inside the corral itself. But still he would snort and back away if any of them tried to touch him.

One night the Boy carried a piece of old rope with him when he came into the corral. After petting and scratching the Horse for a while, he quietly laid the rope over his back. At the first touch of the rope, the Horse bowed his back and crowhopped a time or two to shake it off. But the Boy went on making coaxing noises to him while he scratched his neck and ears, then chirped for

the Horse to follow and walked away, leaving the rope in place.

When the Horse moved, the rope across his back shifted a little, and at first he made a startled side step each time it happened. But by the time the lesson was over, he no longer took any notice even when the dangling ends swung against his sides and legs.

Later when the Boy brought his old saddle blanket from the fence and dropped it on the ground at his feet, the Horse sniffed it curiously but seemed unafraid. So after a while the Boy dragged the box up and set it beside the Horse and, standing on it, he carefully laid the blanket over his back, chirping and crooning as he smoothed out the wrinkles with his hands. The Horse snuffed softly, turning his head to sniff and nibble at the blanket's edge, but stood where he was.

When the Horse had relaxed and started nuzzling the Boy's pockets for some bits of apple he was carrying, the Boy fed them to him one at a time, rubbing his head and muzzle between bites.

From then on the Blind Horse's training went ahead at a faster pace. Getting the big saddle in place the first time took several tries. No matter how carefully the Boy moved, the cinch rings rattled a little, or the stirrup straps creaked, startling the Horse so that he'd move away from the box the Boy was standing on. But after a little coaxing he would come close again, and at last he stood without moving while the Boy set the saddle carefully in place on his back.

Each evening, for a while, the Boy put the saddle on the Horse, but without fastening the cinch, and led him around the corral until he no longer objected to the weight on his back or the sounds of the swinging buckles.

One night when the Ranch Owner and the Horsebreaker came to the corral, they found the Boy in the saddle, riding the Blind Outlaw slowly around inside the fence without bridle or hackamore. How he guided the Horse they could not

tell. But while they watched, the two started, stopped, and turned this way or that as if avoiding unseen obstacles.

"Well! What do you know!" the Ranch Owner remarked after a while. "It looks like the Boy's got himself a Horse!"

"I didn't believe it could be done, but it sure looks like he's got that Horse gentled," the Horsebreaker agreed.

The Boy had been listening but, as usual, saying nothing. Now he grinned a big grin and, chirping softly to the Horse, urged him toward where the men sat on the top rail and stopped him directly below them. The Horse, with his neck stretched to sniff uneasily at the men, snorted and backed away when the Ranch Owner reached down to touch his muzzle, then stood quietly, just beyond the man's reach.

"Looks like he's going to be a one-man horse," the Horsebreaker said, watching as the Boy coaxed the Horse back to where they sat.

For a while longer they watched while the Boy

made birdlike sounds to the Horse as he unsaddled him.

"Well, he's your Horse, Boy," the Ranch Owner told him. "I'll give you a bill of sale whenever you want."

Then after watching the Horse a little longer, he and the Horsebreaker climbed down from the fence and went off into the deepening dusk. When the men were gone, the Boy fed the Horse some bits of dried apple, then after a while he took off his boots and got into his bedroll.

The Horse came up to blow his warm breath softly on the Boy's face, then after cocking his ears to catch the magpie's sleepy complaints from the top of a corral post, settled down to sleep where he stood.

9
The
Roundup

Even though the Boy had gentled the Blind Outlaw and could ride him around inside the corral either bareback or with the saddle, the Horse still had much to learn before he would be a useful saddle horse. So night after night, when the days' chores were finished, the lessons went on.

Each evening when the Boy came to the corral after supper, he found the Blind Horse waiting for him at the gate. At the first sound of the Boy's voice and footsteps, he'd nicker softly and poke his nose between the planks to nuzzle the Boy's hands as he unfastened the heavy latch.

While the Horse sniffed and nudged his pockets, the Boy would make soft conversational sounds and scratch and stroke his head and neck. And when he'd given him the last crumb, he'd saddle the Horse or simply ride him bareback, and the lessons would begin.

As he rode at a slow walk around the corral, the sound of the Boy's soft voice went on and on. Without a bridle, he apparently guided the Horse only by the little chirps and clucks or the light pressure of one knee or the other against his sides. It was impossible for a bystander to tell what the signals were, but the Horse was rapidly learning to understand what was wanted.

At first he occasionally misunderstood a signal to stop or turn, and bumped into the corral or the water trough. But as time went on, this happened less and less often.

Then one night, after he saddled the Horse, the Boy scattered some buckets and a box or two

on the ground inside the corral. Mounting, he rode slowly toward the nearest bucket. When they were close, he used a slight pressure of his knee to guide the Horse around it. But the Blind Horse's attention had apparently wandered and, instead of making the slight turn, he took another step forward and struck the thing with his hoof. At the sound he snorted sharply, throwing up his head and stepping back.

The Boy petted and soothed him, then urged him gently forward until he was close enough to stretch his neck forward and sniff the thing he'd stumbled against. When he'd satisfied himself that it was harmless, he walked safely around it, guided by the Boy's small signals.

From then on the Horse seemed to pay closer attention and, before the evening was over, the Boy could ride him straight to the fence and stop him just before his head touched it, or turn him inches before his hoof touched one of the scattered boxes or buckets.

For several nights, the Boy seemed content to

simply repeat that first night's lessons, riding in zigzags among the scattered boxes and buckets in the corral. But as the Horse's confidence increased, the lessons were moved out into the big stable yard. Constantly chirping and crooning to the Horse, the Boy rode him slowly among the wagons and machinery, around the woodpile, and finally to the big water tank beside the windmill. As the Horse sensed each new obstacle before him, the Boy let him stop and sniff it thoroughly before guiding him past.

And when the Horse would go without hesitation through the narrow space between a hayrack and mowing machine, or even through the alleyway down the center of the horse stable, the Boy began taking him out into the horse pasture where the saddle horses were kept. Here there were small patches of buckbrush, and deepworn stock paths to be avoided, and a little creek to be crossed and recrossed.

Up to now the Horse's habit had been to travel at a careful walk except when frightened, carefully sniffing and testing the ground in front of him before each step. But as he learned to trust the Boy's voice and touch to warn him of things in his way, he became more confident. And sometimes on flat ground, the Boy could even urge him to a trot for a short distance.

By late summer the Boy was regularly riding the Blind Horse instead of the old one when he wrangled the saddle horses in the mornings or rode about the range checking water holes and springs. And by that time the Horse had become somewhat of a pet around the ranch. The cowboys, even the Ranch Owner and the Horsebreaker, had gotten in the habit of carrying bits and pieces from the kitchen for him. He'd take these things from their hands and sniff and nuzzle their pockets looking for more—but still would let no one but the Boy put a hand on him.

When time came for the fall roundup it was decided that the Boy would go along to help the Horse Wrangler and the Cook. So the morning the crew was to leave the ranch, he threw his

bedroll into the chuck wagon with the others, then saddled the Blind Horse and rode out to help the Wrangler with the extra horses.

When they reached the first camping place, he helped unhitch the team from the chuck wagon and turn them into the remuda. Then, while the Wrangler took them out to graze, he went to help the Cook.

After carrying water, filling all the empty buckets, he got on his Horse and rode along the creek looking for firewood. Looping his old throw rope around dry branches and dead small tree trunks, he dragged them to a pile close to where the Cook was setting up his kettles and Dutch ovens.

At first the Horse snorted and skittered away from the feel of the rope over his haunches and the sound of the wood dragging behind. But he soon quieted, and after that made no objections.

When the pile seemed big enough, the Boy took the ax from the wagon and started chopping wood for the cook fire. But the Horse insisted on following him around, kicking dust into the Cook's Dutch ovens and upsetting his kettles, so the Boy got a picket pin and staked him out on a patch of good grass nearby.

As the roundup went on, both the Boy and the Blind Horse more than earned their keep. When the wagon was moved every day or two, as different parts of the range were combed for cattle, the Boy helped the Wrangler with the remuda. And always there was wood to be dragged for the Cook's fires, and water to be carried. When the Boy wasn't riding the Blind Horse, he still kept him picketed on some patch of good grass instead of turning him out with the loose horses, but otherwise there seemed to be nothing unusual about either of them.

In the beginning the men from other ranches were surprised to find that the Boy couldn't talk, and that his Horse was blind. But they soon got used to the idea and no longer seemed to feel that they were anything out of the ordinary. However, being expert horsemen themselves, they were impressed when they heard that the Horse had been an outlaw, and in the evenings one after another told stories of outlaw horses they'd known. But few if any had ever heard of anyone dealing with a horse that was both outlaw and blind.

10
To
Oklahoma

AFTER the roundup was over, the work around the ranch settled back to the usual routine. Besides his daily chores, the Boy helped the Roundup Cook clean his kettles and Dutch ovens and put the big chuck wagon box away for the winter.

Some days he worked with the crews cutting and stacking wild hay on the flats across the river, or helped repair and strengthen the miles of barbwire fence. But wherever he went now, he rode the Blind Horse.

He spent much of his spare time making small repairs on his old, almost unrepairable saddle. The Horse would stand over him, interestedly listening to the soft crooning that went on and on, or reaching his head down to nuzzle the Boy's hands and the straps he was working on.

The young coyote had been disappearing for a few days at a time, and now seemed to have gone away for good. But the tame magpie was still around. He'd perch a while on the Boy's shoulder, apparently listening to his voice, then fly up to a higher lookout on the Horse's back. A few minutes later, they might hear him up by the ranch house, squalling at the dogs as he picked up scraps from around their feed pans.

The feel of the fall was in the air and, at the first faint sound of the wild geese flying in their great wavering vees high overhead, the Boy would stop his work and watch until they were out of sight, beyond the ridge to the south.

"The Boy's getting restless," the Horsebreaker remarked to the Ranch Owner one morning

when flock after flock of the geese were flying overhead in almost endless procession.

"I recognize the signs," the Ranch Owner agreed. "He's about ready to start drifting again."

A few days later a Horse Buyer in a spring wagon, with two riders driving a small bunch of loose horses behind him, drove into the ranch. After some talk with the Ranch Owner, the horses were turned into the big pasture and the riders threw their bedrolls into the bunkhouse.

The strangers stayed for several days while the Horse Buyer visited nearby ranches, looking at horses. Evenings the Boy listened to their talk of places they'd been, and of Oklahoma where they would probably go to sell their horses. When they brought in new ones the Horse Buyer had bought, the Boy always managed to be on hand to help corral them, and to see that the big water trough at the windmill was full.

After the strangers had gotten used to his strange ways and the magpie that was always with him, they found that, in spite of his small size, the Boy was very knowledgeable about handling range stock. So it was not surprising that, when the Horse Buyer began talking of moving on, he asked the Boy if he'd like to go along and help with the horses.

The Boy grinned and nodded. And later, after the Horse Buyer had talked to the Ranch Owner, it was decided. During the winter there wouldn't be much for him to do around the ranch and, if he wanted to see more of the country, this was as good a chance as any.

The Ranch Owner, the Horsebreaker, and the Horse Buyer discussed the difficulty of writing a Bill of Sale for an unbranded horse to a boy who had no name. But in the end they decided that the fact that the Horse was blind and the Boy couldn't speak was identification enough to satisfy any reasonable stock inspector. And so it was done. When finally written out the paper read:

SOLD THIS DAY, ONE UNBRANDED BLIND HORSE,
BLUE-GRAY IN COLOR AND ABOUT FIVE (5) YEARS
OLD, TO A BOY OF SMALL SIZE WHOSE NAME AND
AGE ARE UNKNOWN BECAUSE OF THE FACT THAT
HE CANNOT SPEAK.

> *(signed)* THE RANCH OWNER
> *Witness* . . . THE HORSEBREAKER
> *Witness* . . . THE HORSE BUYER

"There's your Bill of Sale, Boy," the Ranch Owner said. "The Horse is all yours."

The Boy grinned, folded the paper without reading it, and stuck it in his pocket.

Since the Boy had simply stayed on when the Old Buggy Salesman left, there had never been anything said about wages. So now the Ranch Owner gave him a ten-dollar bill and five silver dollars besides the Bill of Sale. Then looking at the torn-up old saddle on the Blind Horse, he said, "Why don't you leave that old hull here and take that spare one hanging in the stable? Some grub-line rider left it a year ago and has never been back."

That saddle was not new, but it was a Furstnow from Miles City, and in much better condition than the Boy's old one, and did much to improve the appearance of the Blind Horse when the change had been made. And while the Boy was shortening the stirrups to fit him, the Horsebreaker was rummaging through his war sack in the bunkhouse and brought out a somewhat ragged sheepskin coat and a well-worn but still serviceable blue flannel shirt.

"They ain't new," he said. "But they'll come in handy on the way to Oklahoma."

The boy grinned and put them in his skimpy bedroll, along with the well-used Indian blanket another of the riders had given him.

So at daybreak one morning the Boy threw his bedroll into the Horse Buyer's spring wagon and put his new saddle on the Blind Horse. Then with the magpie on his shoulder, and driving the old potbellied horse ahead of him, he rode out to

help bunch the ones he would help drive south, perhaps all the way to Oklahoma.

At the top of the ridge to the south, the Boy turned in his saddle and raised a hand to the Ranch Owner and the cowboys still standing by the gate. And that was the last they saw or heard of either the Boy or the Blind Outlaw.

But there are grizzled old-timers in that country who still remember the unnamed Boy who couldn't speak, and the Blind Outlaw Horse he gentled during that summer so long ago.